S0-BYP-603

9

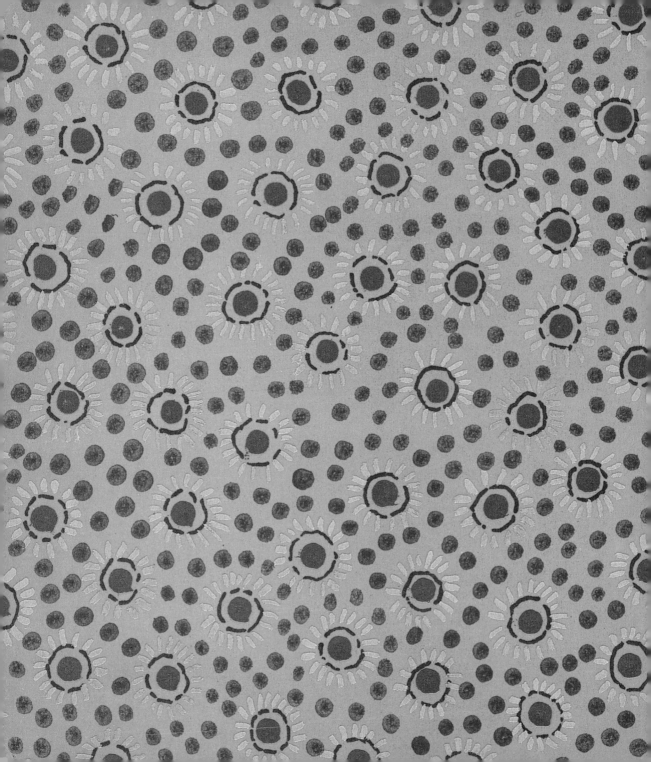

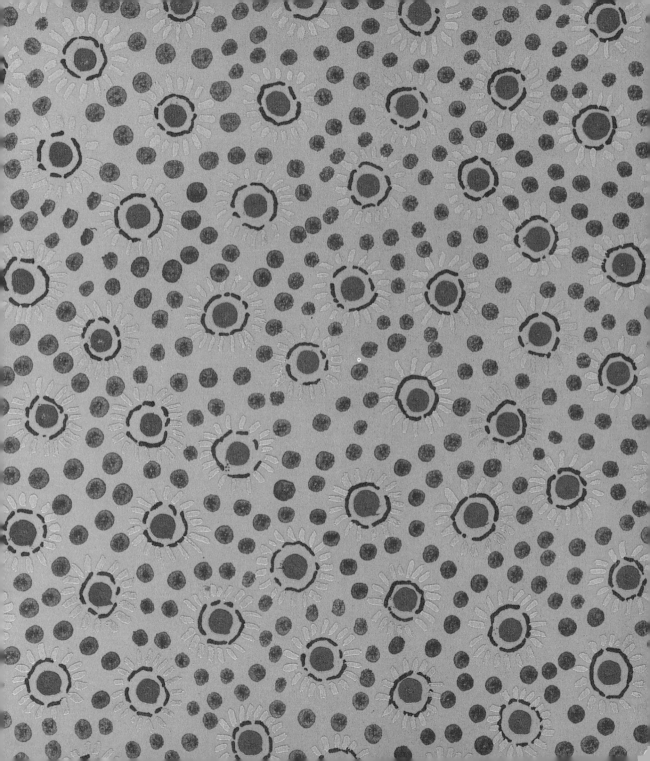

D.W.'s Lost Blankie

Marc Brown

Little, Brown and Company

Boston   New York   London

For Eliza

First Edition

Based on a teleplay by Tom Hertz

D.W.™is a trademark of Marc Brown

Library of Congress Cataloging-in-Publication Data

Brown, Marc Tolon.
    D.W.'s lost blankie / Marc Brown. — 1st ed.
      p.   cm.
    Summary: When D.W. cannot find her special blanket, Arthur and Dad
try to help her, but with no success, until Mom saves the day.
    ISBN 0-316-10914-2 (hc)   ISBN 0-316-11595-9 (pb)
    [1. Blankets — Fiction. 2. Family life — Fiction. 3. Aardvark —
Fiction. I. Title.]
PZ7.B81618Dys 1996
[E] — dc21   97-6944
            HC: 10 9 8 7 6 5 4 3 2 1
            PB: 10 9 8 7 6 5 4 3 2 1

WOR

Printed in the United States of America

D.W. and Blankie have been together forever.

Blankie was there when she learned to eat by herself,

when she got her first tooth,

when she learned to walk,

and at all her birthdays.

"With Blankie," said D.W., "I can fall asleep just like that. It's better than a night-light."

One day D.W. came home from day care and looked in her special Blankie hiding place.

"My blankie's gone!" she screamed.

Everyone helped D.W. look for Blankie.
Father looked on top of things.
D.W. looked under things.
Arthur looked in things.

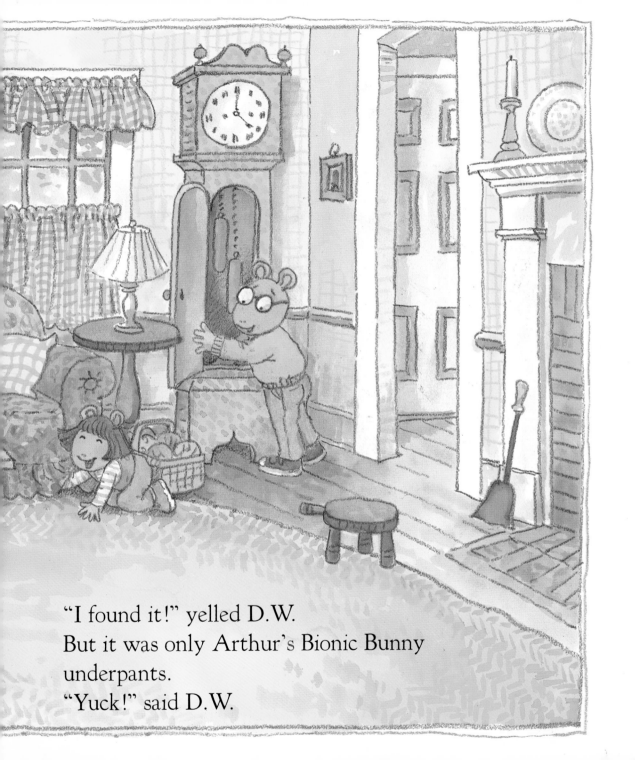

"I found it!" yelled D.W.
But it was only Arthur's Bionic Bunny
underpants.
"Yuck!" said D.W.

"Think," said Arthur. "When did you last have it?"
"I think I had it at the playground this morning," said
D.W. "The Tibble twins wanted it. Maybe they broke into
the house while I was at day care and stole my blankie!"
"There's just one problem," said Arthur. "They were at
day care with you."

"Wait!" said D.W. "I know exactly where it is. Blankie's at
the library. I think it went down the slot when Mommy
and I returned our books."

Ms. Turner checked the Lost and Found.
"Sorry, honey, no blankies," she said.
"Thanks for checking," said Arthur.

"Now I remember!" said D.W. "Blankie's at the car wash."

"When the big vacuum thingie came down," said D.W. "I closed my eyes and it sucked Blankie out the window."
"It only sucks up water," explained the car wash attendant.

"You're welcome to one of my polishing cloths."
"It's not dirty enough," said Arthur. "Thanks anyway."
"Blankie's gone forever," whined D.W. on the way home.

D.W. was unusually quiet the rest of the day.
When Arthur wanted to watch the *Bionic Bunny Show*,
she didn't yell, "I want to watch the *Pretty Pony Show!*"
the way she did every other night.
"I sure hope you find your blankie soon," said Arthur.
"This is spooky."

"Time for bed," said Father.

"I can't sleep without Blankie!" sobbed D.W.

"Try," said Father. "When Mom gets home, she'll help me find it."

He kissed D.W. good night.

D.W. tried to close her eyes, but they kept popping open.
She missed Blankie and she felt sad.
She thought about how Blankie always made her feel better.
That made her feel worse.

Just then the door opened.

"I have something for you," said Mother.

"Kisses and hugs won't help," moaned D.W.

"It's your blankie," said Mother. "I found it."

"Blankie!" cried D.W. "Hey . . . this isn't my blankie. . . ."

"Yes, it is," said Mother. "I washed it."

"You killed it!" said D.W.

Mother gave D.W. a kiss and hug good night.

"Sleep tight," she said. "I love you."

D.W. didn't say anything.

Blankie didn't smell quite the same or look the same.

D.W. put Blankie to her cheek.
"I love you, Blankie," she whispered.
D.W. decided to be extra-nice to Mom at breakfast,
right after she found a new place to hide Blankie.
Then she fell asleep, just like that.

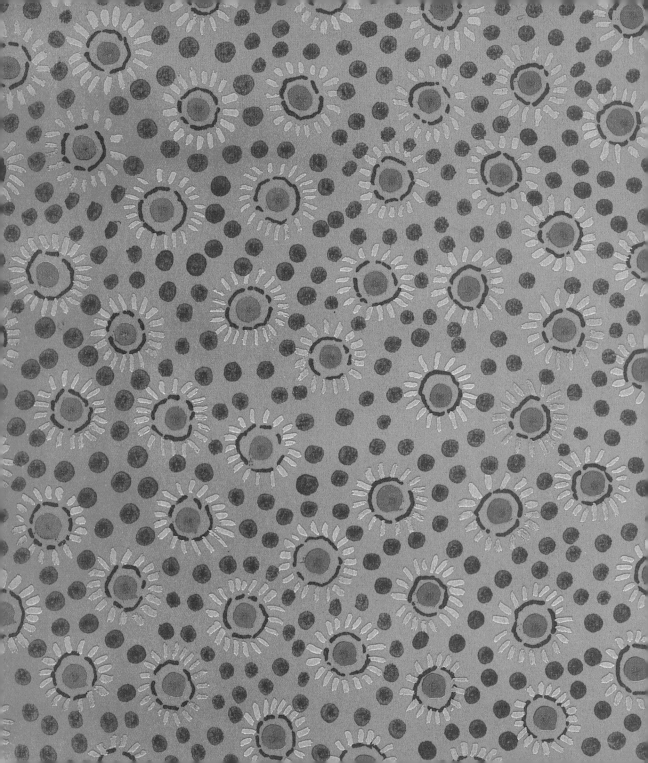

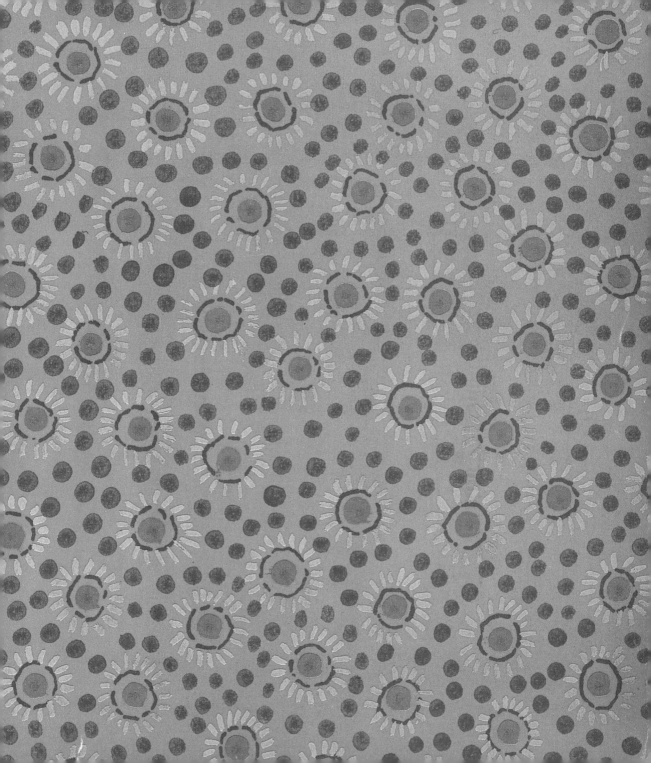